What Do You Remember?

for Katy, Anna and Jack

Text copyright © 2002 by Paul Stewart. Illustration copyright © 2002 by Chris Riddell
This paperback edition first published in 2003 by Andersen Press Ltd.
The rights of Paul Stewart and Chris Riddell to be identified as the author and illustrator of this work
have been asserted by them in accordance with the Copyright, Designs and Patents Act, 1988.
First published in Great Britain in 2003 by Andersen Press Ltd. 20 Vauxhall Bridge Road, London SW1V 2SA.
Published in Australia by Random House Australia Pty., 20 Alfred Street, Milsons Point, Sydney, NSW 2061.
All rights reserved. Colour separated in Italy by Fotoriproduzioni Grafiche, Verona.
Printed and bound in Italy by Grafiche AZ, Verona.

10 9 8 7 6 5 4 3 2 1

British Library Cataloguing in Publication Data available.

ISBN 1 84270 229 7

This book has been printed on acid-free paper

What Do You Remember?

by Paul Stewart
with pictures by Chris Riddell

Ⓐ

Andersen Press
London

"RABBIT," said Hedgehog. "Let's play 'Remembering'."
"I don't want to," said Rabbit. "You know what always happens."
"*Please*, Rabbit," said Hedgehog. "It won't happen this time. I promise."
"Oh, all right," said Rabbit. "If you promise."

"Close your eyes," said Hedgehog.
Rabbit closed his eyes.
Hedgehog led him away.

"Where do you think we are?" said Hedgehog.
Rabbit twitched his nose. The air smelled damp
and leafy. "I think we're in the wood," he said.

"Open your eyes!" said Hedgehog.
Rabbit opened his eyes. They *were* in the wood.

"June, July, September, what do you remember?" said Hedgehog.
"I . . . I remember . . ." Rabbit began.

"You climbed on to the tree-stump," said Hedgehog excitedly. "You wobbled about. Like this." "No," said Rabbit, a little hurt. "I was *dancing*."

"Then you fell off," said Hedgehog.
"I *jumped*," said Rabbit.

"My turn," said Hedgehog. He closed his eyes.
Rabbit led him out of the woods.

At the top of the ridge, he stopped and placed
an acorn in Hedgehog's paw.
"Open your eyes," he said.
"Say the rhyme," said Hedgehog.
"June, July, September, what do you remember?"
said Rabbit.

"We each had an acorn," said Hedgehog, "just like this one. We had an acorn-rolling competition." He turned to Rabbit. "You kept dropping yours."

"I was bouncing it," said Rabbit very quietly.
"Rabbit," said Hedgehog, "that was too easy.
I want another go."

Hedgehog closed his eyes again. Rabbit took him
down to the stepping-stones.

"Well?" said Rabbit.
"You've forgotten the rhyme again," said Hedgehog.
"June, July, September," said Rabbit rather impatiently.
"What do you remember?"

Hedgehog jumped on to the
first stepping-stone.
"I remember a hot,
dry day," he said.
"The stream was low.
We crossed to the island –
and you nearly fell in."

"I didn't!" said Rabbit.
"You tripped," said Hedgehog.
"I caught you."
"I was picking up a water-snail,"
said Rabbit. "For *you*."

"I don't remember
a water-snail,"
said Hedgehog.

"I dropped it,"
said Rabbit.
"When you
grabbed me."

Hedgehog jumped to the second stepping-stone.
"No, no, Rabbit," he said.
"You've got it all wrong again."

"Oh, Hedgehog!" said Rabbit crossly.
"This is what always happens when
we play 'Remembering'.
And you promised it wouldn't!
You get all bossy and showy-offy.
You tell me my memories
are wrong."

"But they *are* wrong,"
said Hedgehog.
"You did trip.
I did catch you."

"*Hmmph!*"
said Rabbit.

Rabbit turned his back on
Hedgehog.
He sat on the ground.
He folded his arms.
"It's not *my* fault that you're so
full of forget," said Hedgehog.

"I'm not listening," said Rabbit.
He put his paws over his ears.
"*Hm, hm, hm, hm,*"
he hummed.

"I REMEMBER *EVERYTHING!*"
Hedgehog shouted.
He turned and jumped to the
third stepping-stone, and . . .

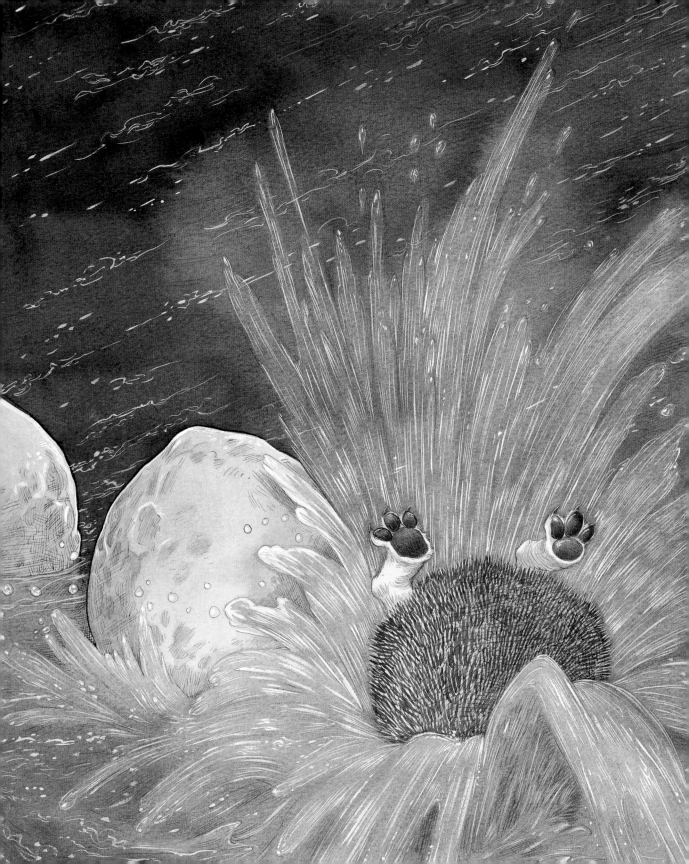

SPLASH!

Rabbit jumped up. "Oh, Hedgehog!" he said, as he hurried to help him. "You forgot that the third stepping-stone wobbles."

"You're right," said Hedgehog. "So I didn't remember *everything* after all."

"I'm sorry I got cross," said Rabbit.

"I'm sorry I *made* you cross," said Hedgehog.

"Well, I'm sorry I made you make me cross," said Rabbit.

"Rabbit," said Hedgehog. "Can we be friends again?"
"Of course we can, Hedgehog!" said Rabbit.
"*Best* friends."

"Hedgehog," said Rabbit. "There is something I really don't remember. I don't remember the first time we met. Do you?"

Hedgehog thought. And thought and thought.

He sucked his paw and scratched his head.

"No, Rabbit," he said at last. "That is something I don't remember. I feel as if I've known you for ever."

Rabbit nodded. "That's just how I feel, Hedgehog," he said. "For ever and ever."

Stories about Rabbit and Hedgehog

"Rabbit and Hedgehog are a winning pair."
Wendy Cope in the *Daily Telegraph*

A Little Bit of Winter
Hardback ISBN 0 86264 814 9
Paperback ISBN 0 86264 998 6

The Birthday Presents
Hardback ISBN 0 86264 892 0
Paperback ISBN 1 84270 035 9

Rabbit's Wish
Hardback ISBN 0 86264 719 3
Paperback ISBN 1 84270 089 8

What Do You Remember?
Hardback ISBN 1 84270 080 4
Paperback ISBN 1 84270 229 7